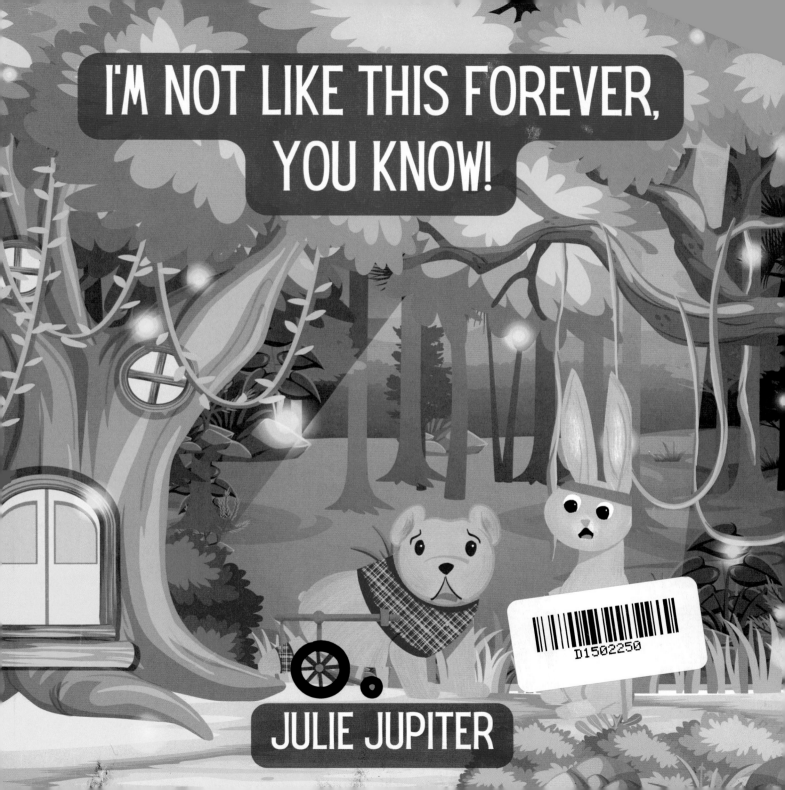

For extraordinary friends

Copyright © 2023 by Julie Jupiter

All rights reserved. No portion of this book may be reproduced, stored in a retrieval system, or transmitted in any form by any means—electronic, mechanical, photocopy, recording, scanning, or other—except for brief quotations in critical reviews or articles, without the prior written permission of the publisher.

Printed in the United States of America

This is a work of fiction. Names, characters, places, and incidents either are the product of the author's imagination or are used fictitiously. Any resemblance to actual persons, living or dead, events, or locales is entirely coincidental.

ISBN: 979-8-3602-6960-1
Library of Congress Control Number: 2023907846

Published by Julie Jupiter Book Club
Irving, Texas
www.juliejupiterbookclub.com

I am a rabbit, and I love to hop and run.

| forest | Rabbit | Fox | Raccoon | run | 3 |

I hop when I run, and I flop when I'm done.

4 | forest | Rabbit | Fox | hop | run

I hop, hop, hop, over the hills,
under the branches,
and through the hollow logs.

| tree | log | happy | sad | mad | 5 |

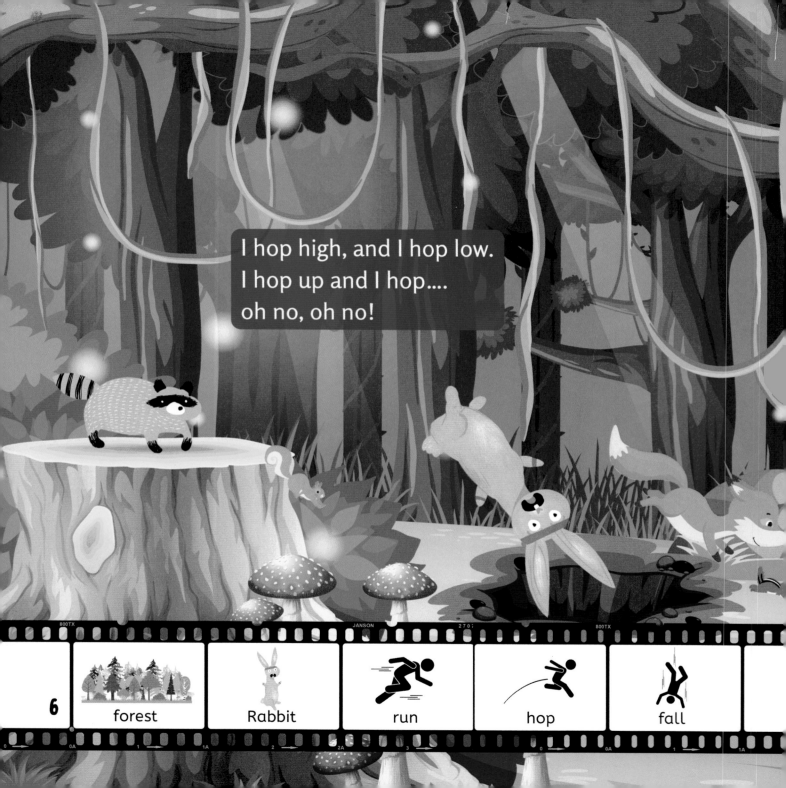

I hop high, and I hop low.
I hop up and I hop....
oh no, oh no!

6 | forest | Rabbit | run | hop | fall

Oh no.

| stump | hole | happy | sad | mad | 7 |

No, Rabbit. You're too slow.

But I'm not like this forever, you know!

| crutches | bandage | happy | sad | mad | 9 |

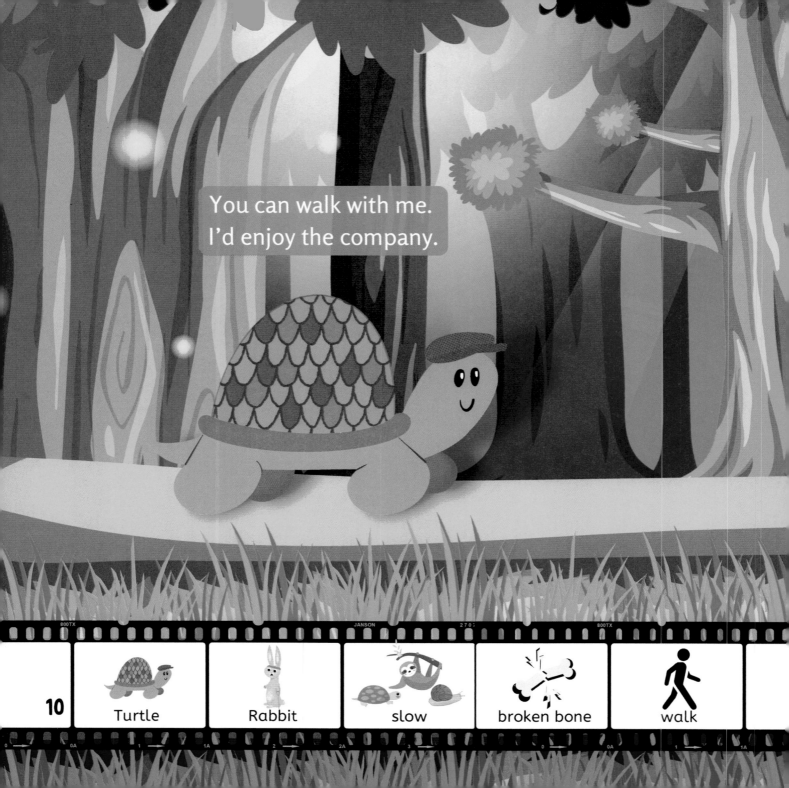

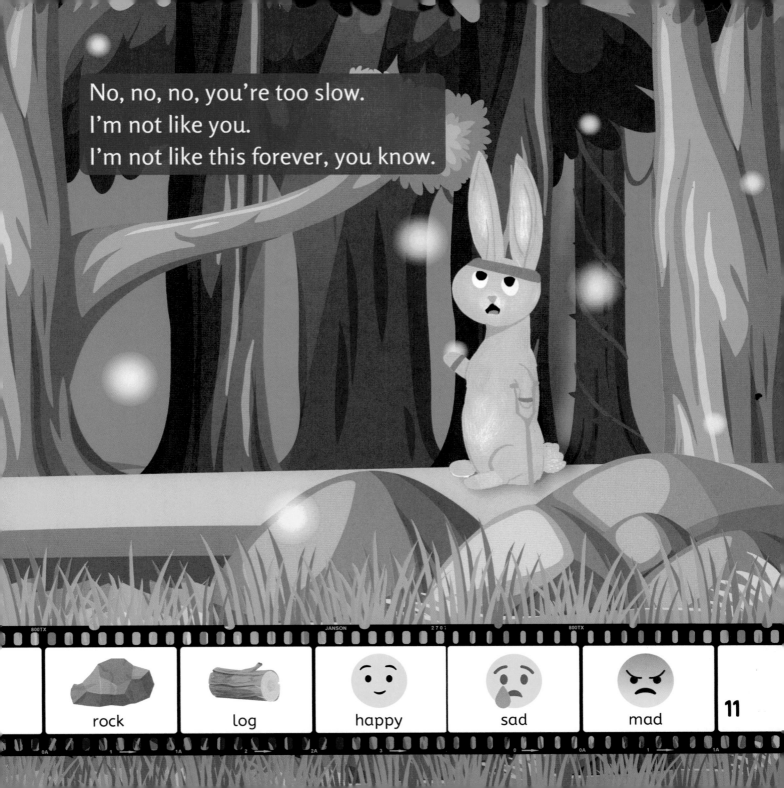

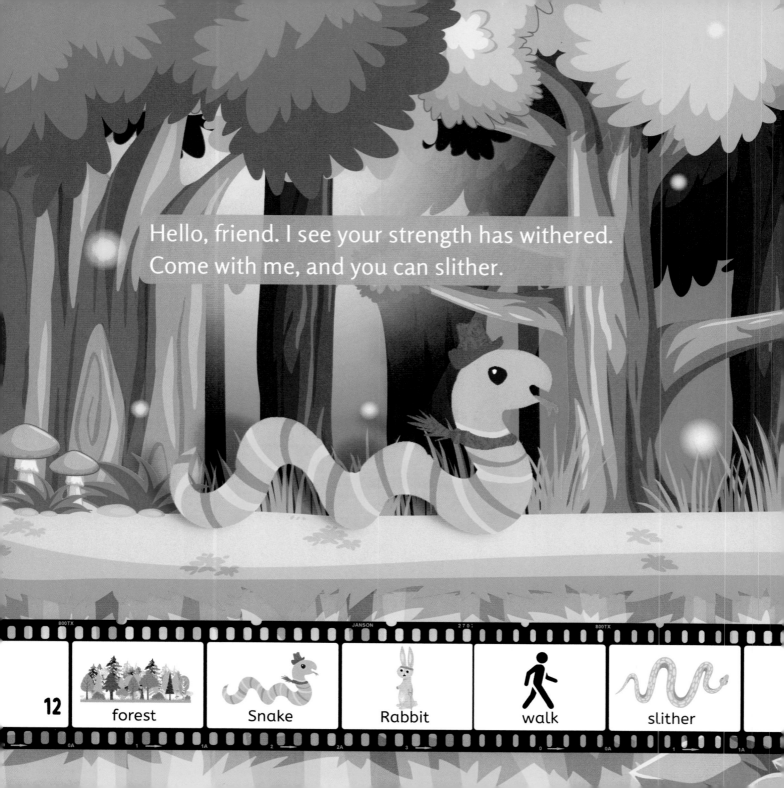

Hello, friend. I see your strength has withered. Come with me, and you can slither.

forest | Snake | Rabbit | walk | slither

No, no, you don't even have legs to go.
I appreciate the offer, but I'm not like you.
I'm not like this forever, you know.

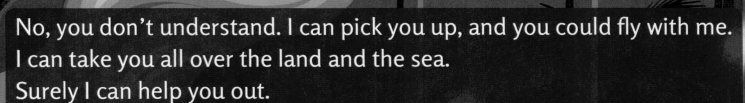

No, you don't understand. I can pick you up, and you could fly with me.
I can take you all over the land and the sea.
Surely I can help you out.
Flying is even faster than running or hopping, no doubt.

No thank you. I have somewhere to go.
I'm not like this forever, you know.

mushrooms

friends

scared

sad

mad

15

Well hello Rabbit! I'm out for my walk.
It's good to keep fit and keep going.
Would you like to come with me?
You can walk, and I'll be rolling.

16 | Dog | Rabbit | pet wheelchair | roll | walk

So long, Rabbit! Keep in touch! We're so sorry you can't keep up!

18 | Rabbit | Turtle | Squirrel | Raccoon | rest

I thought I was so quick and clever.
But what if I'm like this forever?

| fast | slow | happy | sad | mad | 19 |

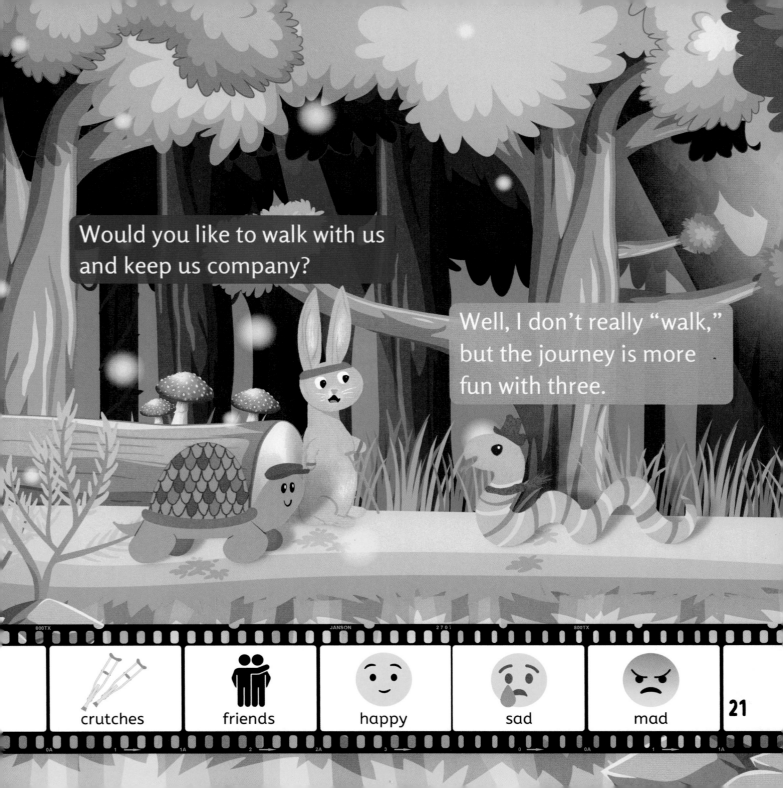

Does anybody want a ride,
way up in the air?
There's room on my wings for all of you.
We can go anywhere!

| Rabbit | Turtle | Hawk | Snake | Dog |

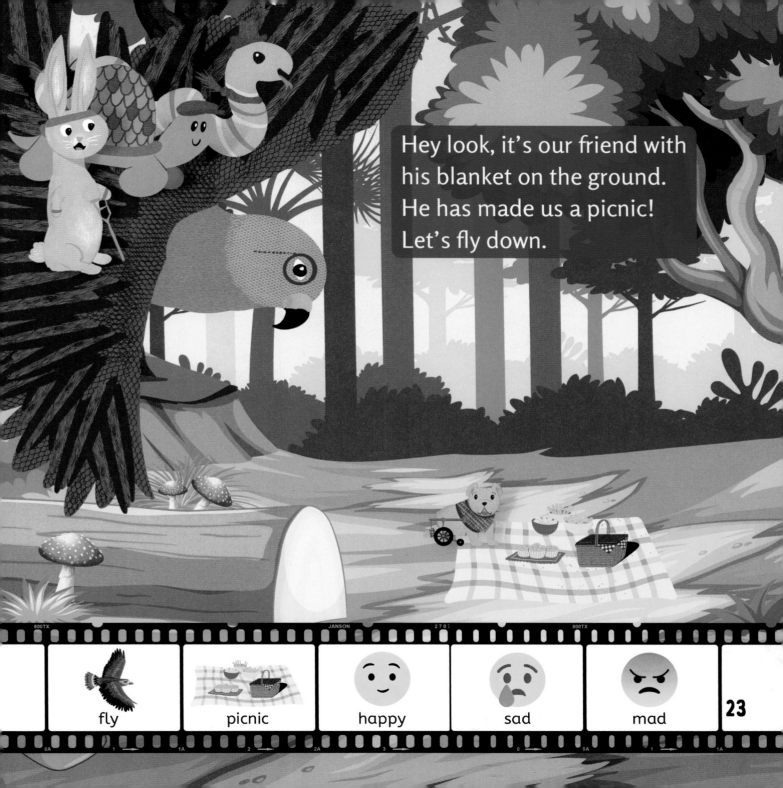

Hey look, it's our friend with his blanket on the ground. He has made us a picnic! Let's fly down.

fly	picnic	happy	sad	mad

23

friends	picnic	happy	sad	mad

? Discuss the Story

NOTE: Some questions may have multiple correct answers. Questions are meant to encourage communication.

1. Who is the main character?
2. Where does the story take place? What is the setting?
3. What does Rabbit like to do?
4. What is the problem in the story?
5. How did Rabbit feel when he fell in the hole?
6. What does the Rabbit use when he gets hurt?
7. What can the new friends do together?
8. Where did the animals go at the end?
9. How does Rabbit feel at the end of the story?
10. Did you like the story?

I'M NOT LIKE THIS FOREVER, YOU KNOW!

COMMUNICATION BOARD

what	I/me	yes	no	happy
who	Rabbit	like	don't like	sad
where	Dog	run	walk	forest
when	Turtle	jump	feel	crutches
how much	Hawk	fall	say	picnic

Parents and educators may photocopy this page to create flexible learning opportunities for the home or classroom.

Discuss the Characters
"Who" Questions

NOTE: Some questions may have multiple correct answers. Questions are meant to encourage communication.

1. In the story, who gets hurt?
2. Who is fast?
3. Who is slow?
4. Who can slither?
5. Who can fly?
6. Who can jump?
7. Who can roll?
8. Who has hurt feelings?
9. Who changes in the story?
10. Who is Rabbit's friend?

CHARACTERS
COMMUNICATION BOARD

Rabbit

Dog

Turtle

Hawk

Snake

Fox

Parents and educators may photocopy this page to create flexible learning opportunities for the home or classroom.

❓ Discuss Forest Animals

NOTE: Some questions may have multiple correct answers. Questions are meant to encourage communication.

1. Which animals have tails?
2. Which animals can fly?
3. Which animals have antlers?
4. Which animals can jump far?
5. Which animals have pointy, sharp spines or quills?
6. Which animals have feathers?
7. Which animals have four legs?
8. Which animals are larger than a person?
9. Which animals are smaller than a basketball?
10. Which animal would you like to have as a pet?

FOREST PLANTS & ANIMALS
COMMUNICATION BOARD

forest	tree	log	tree stump	leaves
acorn	mushrooms	pinecone	owl	hawk
rabbit	squirrel	chipmunk	fox	raccoon
hedgehog	porcupine	beaver	moose	deer
snail	mouse	weasel	wolf	bear

Parents and educators may photocopy this page to create flexible learning opportunities for the home or classroom.

GUIDED COMPREHENSION QUESTIONS

NOTE: Some questions may have multiple correct answers.
Questions are meant to encourage communication.

1. Where do the animals run?

store   doctor's office   forest

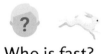

2. Who is fast?

Raccoon   Fox   Dog

3. Who is slow?

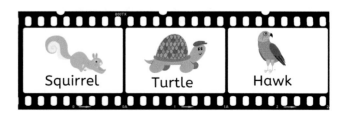

Squirrel   Turtle   Hawk

4. What happens to Rabbit?

fall   broken bone   wheelchair

Parents and educators may photocopy this page to create flexible learning opportunities for the home or classroom.

GUIDED COMPREHENSION QUESTIONS

NOTE: Some questions may have multiple correct answers.
Questions are meant to encourage communication.

5. Who rolls to go?

| Turtle | Rabbit | Dog |

6. How does Hawk go?

| walk | slither | fly |

7. Who is Rabbit's new friend?

| Dog | Raccoon | Snake |

8. What do the new friends have at the end?

| cocoa | cake | picnic |

Parents and educators may photocopy this page to create flexible learning opportunities for the home or classroom.

A GUIDE FOR PARENTS, TEACHERS, AND SLPS

You can use the communication board at the end of the book to ask questions and provide communication options to supplement the vocabulary found on each page of the book. I like to cut out the communication board and laminate it, then attach it to the back with colorful tape or a comb binder.

Model communication when you are asking questions by using the board, pointing to the vocabulary you are using. Here are examples:

Where is Rabbit?   **What is Dog feeling?**

Wh- questions: There are endless "what/which" questions you can ask with the vocabulary on each page:
"What changes Rabbit's mind?"
"What is Fox doing?"
"What does Dog see?"
You can ask "who" questions about different characters in the book. Use the "where" question symbol to ask where they see something on a page. You can ask questions like, "Where is the tree?" or "Where is Turtle?" using the board.

Describing questions: Children can use the communication board to describe what they are reading using thematic vocabulary. They can also use the vocabulary on each page to answer describing questions, such as, "What is in the tree?" or "What could Dog buy?"

Preferences questions: Children can use the communication board to say they "like" or "don't like" something they are reading about.

Yes/No questions: By using the "yes" and "no" pictures on the communication board, you can rephrase many questions to accommodate yes/no responses.

Julie Jupiter Book Club books help children communicate and connect with what they read. Early readers and children with special communication needs can use picture symbols to communicate and share the reading experience with parents, teachers, and friends.

Special education teachers and SLPs can use Julie Jupiter Book Club books to build a rich resource of fringe vocabulary for nonverbal and early readers to communicate along with CORE boards.

Connect with the Julie Jupiter Book Club on **TeachersPayTeachers.com** to find printable versions of books and resources to help children build basic language and learning skills like matching, labeling, sorting, classifying, and reading comprehension.

ABOUT THE AUTHOR

Julie Jupiter is an author, educator, and creator of the Julie Jupiter Book Club. She writes fiction and nonfiction books for early readers and children with special communication needs, using built-in picture communication support. She has also written a suspense thriller novel, *Pig in a Blanket* (under the name Julie Robles). She lives in Dallas, Texas, with her husband and two wild and crazy sons. Julie loves to drink coffee and hear a spooky story on any given dark and stormy night.

Additional printable books with visual communication supports and resources for basic language and learning skills are available at the Julie Jupiter Book Club store at **TeachersPayTeachers.com**.

Get to know me! Be part of the Julie Jupiter Book Club on social media **@JulieJupiterBookClub**. Visit **www.juliejupiterbookclub.com** to see what's coming next from the book club!

Made in the USA
Monee, IL
18 June 2023

35855460R00024